Compsognathus
komp-sog-NATH-us

Elasmosaurus
ee-LAZ-mo-saw-rus

Deinosuchus
dine-o-SOOK-us

Stegosaurus

STEG-o-saw-rus

Hadrosaur

HAD-ro-saw

Archaeopteryx

ark-ee-OPT-er-ix

Ankylosaurus

an-KILL-o-saw-rus

Something roary for Family Story.
To the Williams boys:
Gregory, Luke & Jonny
– T.M.

For my good friends Katka & Alistair,
and whoever might come along
for them to share it with . . .
– L.C.

First published 2010 by Macmillan Children's Books
a division of Macmillan Publishers Limited
20 New Wharf Road, London N1 9RR
Basingstoke and Oxford
Associated companies throughout the world
www.panmacmillan.com

ISBN: 978-0-230-74175-1 (HB)
ISBN: 978-0-330-50676-2 (PB)

Text copyright © Tony Mitton 2010
Illustrations copyright © Lynne Chapman 2010
Moral rights asserted.

www.lynnechapman.co.uk

1 3 5 7 9 8 6 4 2

A CIP catalogue record for this book is available from the British Library.

Printed in China

Rumble, Roar, DINOSAUR!

More prehistoric poems with lift-the-flap surprises!

Written by

Tony Mitton

Illustrated by

Lynne Chapman

MACMILLAN CHILDREN'S BOOKS

We've been extinct for ages . . .

But you can read about us on our very own pages.
Some of us like water, some live on land,
some of us go solo, while some stay in a band.
Some of us munch plants, while others hunt for meat,
so come and see the kinds of things we might have liked to eat.
In this book are many dino-facts you'll want to know.
So take a look and watch us in our world of long ago.

Hadrosaur

A herd of hungry hadrosaurs are honking through the trees,
"Have you found some juicy leaves or munchy pines, please?"
A hadrosaur can signal from the horn upon its head
to say it's found some fodder, so the others can get fed.
The racket in the forest when the hadrosaurs hunt round,
is like a rowdy orchestra, full of booming sound.

Archaeopteryx

Flapping on a branch with a squawk and a shriek,
what a funny bird I am, with teeth in my beak!
I wear three claws on the end of each wing
which shows, deep down, I'm a dinosaur-thing.
But hey, look, I'm feathered, not scaled or furred,
so that must mean I'm the very first bird.
Can I really fly like a bird on the breeze?

Stegosaurus

I am Stegosaurus. Steadily I go,
searching for the place where the best plants grow.
My nut-sized brain in my tiny little head
somehow finds a way to get my heavy body fed.

My back is cluttered up with plates in a line
for cooling and protecting me and helping me look fine.
But when it comes to enemies, not one of them likes
the tip of my tail with its sharp, hard spikes!

Ankylosaurus

When I'm busy feeding I look easy to attack,
but look at all this tough stuff I'm wearing on my back.
You may think me a meal that a carnivore might like,
but imagine trying to chew through a knobble or a spike.
If you mean to eat me, believe me, it's a waste . . .
Even if you caught me, you wouldn't like the taste!

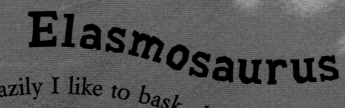

Elasmosaurus

Lazily I like to bask, drifting in the sea,
waiting for my dinner to find its way to me.
My head is very tiny and my neck is like a snake,
and so I'm built just perfectly to strike down and to take
an unsuspecting fish as it swims too near . . .

Deinosuchus

The grandad of all crocodiles, I'm really rather longer –
a crocodile to look at, only bigger and much stronger.

Mind out, other dinosaurs, I wield a wicked bite.

Behind my smile lies waiting a massive appetite.

When I give a cheery grin I may look kind and happy,

but watch out for my jagged jaws – they're seriously . . .

Compsognathus

I'm a tiny dinosaur, scuttling around,
right down here on the hard, dry ground.
Not every dinosaur is built like a wall.
I'm just chicken-sized, really quite small.

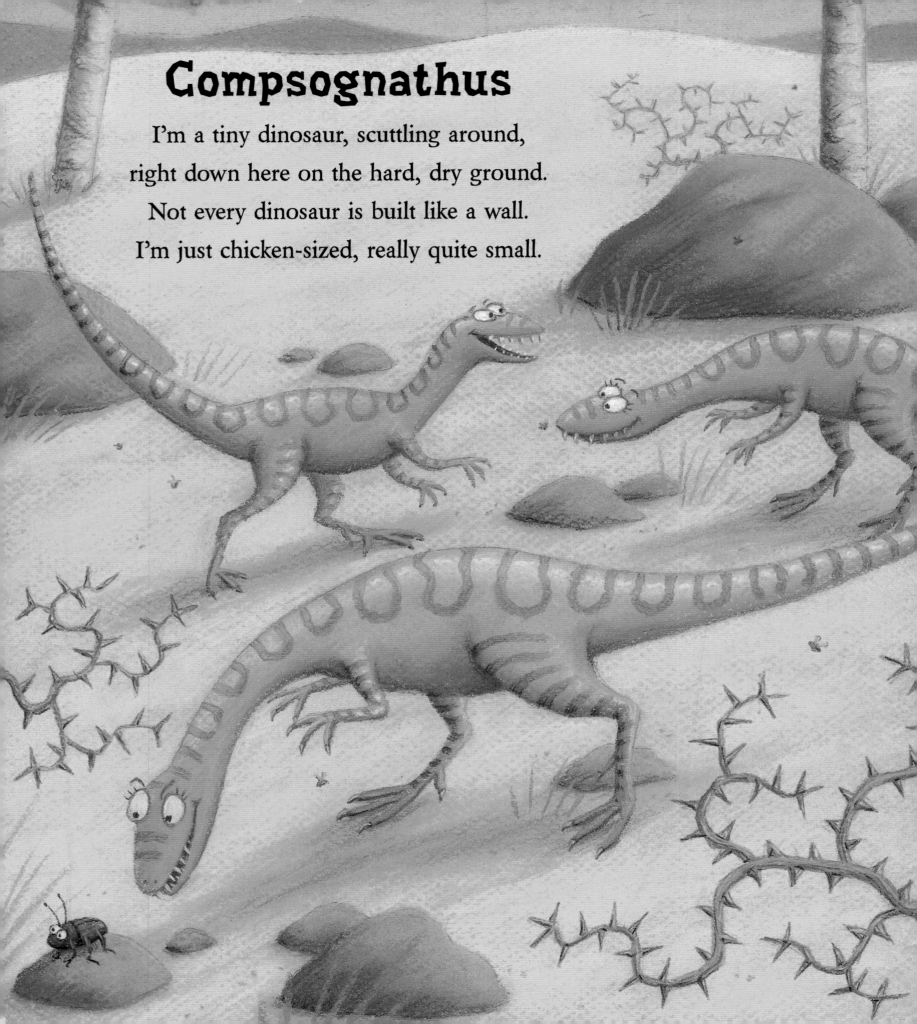

Still, I'm a hunter. I'm sharp and I'm fast.
See that lizard, about to flash past?
He'll be the loser, and I'll be the winner.
That tasty lizard is going to be . . .

Compsognathus
was one of the smallest dinosaurs.
Its name means "pretty jaw".

Elasmosaurus
had a bendy, snake-like neck
that was as long as its body.

Deinosuchus
was like a monster crocodile and
could grow to 16 metres, the length
of one and a half buses!

Stegosaurus

was as heavy as an elephant
but had a brain that was only
the size of a walnut.

Hadrosaur

had a kind of duck-bill and could
honk and hoot through its nose.

Archaeopteryx

means "ancient wing".
It was the first bird.

Ankylosaurus

had a big bony club on the end of its tail,
probably for hitting its predators.